Reviews

"Jason Hess possesses an ability to draw characters pulled directly from real life drastic events; or seemingly, from the headlines of today. Being involved, and a longtime fan of the field of the paranormal, Hess has a unique perspective that intertwines real life and the aspects of the unknown…"

Gian Temperilli – Is the co-author and editor of "Heaven Can You Hear Me?" by late famed FOX "Sightings" televised psychic and legendary paranormal researcher, Peter James. Gian currently co-hosts his daughter's wildly popular weekly broadcast on LiveParanormal.com, "The Ghost Host" with Sophia Temperilli…

~~~
~~~

Reviews

Other books available

*So You Want To Be a Ghost Hunter
*Ghost Hunted *The Beginning* part of the Mike Taylor
Series

More to come….

Paratales:
Paranormal Short Stories
By Jason Hess

Edited by
Kanda Delisle

DragonEye Publishing

Paratales – Paranormal Short Stories
By Jason Hess
Copyright 2013 by Jason Hess

Edited by Kanda Delisle

First Edition
First Printing – June 2013

ISBN 13: 978-1-61500-040-1 Trade Paperback
ISBN 13; 978-1-61500-046-3 (EPub E-Book)
Library of Congress Control Number: 2013902980

Visit our website
www.DragonEyePublishers.com

Published by DragonEye Publishing

DragonEye Publishing
753 Linden Place, Unit A
Elmira, NY 14901 USA

Table of content

Foreword

Jason Hess is a new and upcoming author and is doing very well so far! Jason Hess is a seasoned Paranormal Investigator who has drawn some of his stories from actual experiences while being in Rock Island Paranormal. I have watched him pour himself into his writing and watched the whole process of him completing this book. The stories are definitely enough to keep you interested!

There are six stories in this book and all of them seemed to be more exciting than the one before it. The stories include possession, accidents, haunted items, the all famous Ouija Board, and deceased lovers. I would recommend this book to anybody who loves reading about the paranormal!

Ellen Covemaker-Hess

Paratales
A collection of paranormal short stories

Paratales is a series of short stories that touch on the paranormal. Although most tails were made on first hand accounts they are still purely fiction. They are a slight touch on the dark side but still entertaining for all. Please partake in our little paranormal world full of poltergeist and ghost. Most hauntings are proven to be figments of imagination or have logical explanations. But then there are some that go unexplained. Theses stories are about some of the unexplained and about what those people feel. Have fun reading and please……..don't turn off the lights.

Thanks to Ellyn for believing in me.
Also Mikki, Hailee Ann, and Haylie for their love

1
POSSESED

As I think of my life, I wonder if I could ever understand it. It's a blur.....I cannot determine which is real or not. Now I sit in a room, alone, only a doctor or nurse come in to see me. My family has basically given up on me. My life is hell......and I am only 19 years old.

It started when I was 3 and I saw people all around me. They would talk to me and play. The problem is I was the only one to see them. My parents believed it was imaginary friends that many children have, and never though anything of it except it was cute. And when my friends would break something or do anything wrong I would be blamed. I told them that it was the people but they never did believe. They took me to a doctor to have me checked out thinking it might be a psychological problem, nothing ever showed up. And in time most of those around me went away....except one. But I learned to ignore him, no matter what happened. I took the blame for what he did and then was classified as a troubled child.

Mostly the part which got me here is when I started college....yes I made it through high school. I had very few friends because I was odd. And so…

This could be a fresh start for me, a new life.

The day of orientation was a grim one. I had to get into my dorm room and sign in for all my courses. Needless to say, not get lost on campus. I found my dorm and located my room. A set of bunk beds and two desks made up the furniture in the room. Most of the comfortable furniture was located in the common room where all the people in the dorm could interact with each other and visit with friends. Being in a co-ed dorm was natural to me growing up with a brother and a sister, both older then I. But none of these girls looked like my sister.

As I brought my belongings into my room I noticed I have a room mate. He was kind of a slob….clothing scattered over the top bunk and boxes half opened in the corner. Well maybe my example would rub off on him. I am what many may consider a neat freak….but I had to keep up with the people around me so I wouldn't get into trouble back home. Inside the closet contained two sets of drawers, a makeshift dresser and the clothes could be hung on a bar above it. So that should be a good place to start.

I was about half way done putting my clothes away when someone walked in.

"Hey! I'm Tony," which was short for Antonio, "You must be Brian."

"How did you know? I didn't even know I had a roommate."

"Well you do, and I am him. Check your orientation sheets, it's on there. Man, am I like the only person without a laptop around here. What kind of games you have for this thing?"

Games? I am not really a gamer at all. I use my computer mostly to surf the internet. Get into chat rooms, check my favorite websites and stay in contact with my friends. "I didn't bring any." Now I wondered if he would then exclude me and treat me like an orphan or blow it off. Hell, it's my computer and I just met him. Did he think I would just let him play around with it or what?

"Oh….anyway this machine looks like it cost a lot. How much did you pay for this bra?" said Tony with a grin on his face.

Well this was looking up. I made my first friend here. So I stopped unpacking so I could talk to Tony eye to eye. Tony was a rather short guy….around 5'4" and slim. You can look at him and tell he was athletic. Short black hair with similar eyes and a smile that I don't think ever left his face. I myself am no slouch. I'm 5'10" around 170….maybe a little out of shape but I never was really into sports. But I tried to stay healthy. I always though personal hygiene was important, and I kept my hair short and well groomed. But I did have a bad habit of biting my nails; they looked like I trimmed them with a chainsaw.

"I couldn't really tell you. My grandmother bought it for me as a graduation present. Actually she gave me one that barely could do anything so I returned it and use the money I had saved to get this one. It's pretty fast but I need to bump the memory up a bit." God, am I coming across as a computer nerd now? I just looked down to the floor thinking I ruined a good friendship before it started.

"Well go get some extra ram and we will get it going." said Tony to my surprise. "I could get this thing surfing at light speed if you want. My pc should be delivered soon. I just couldn't get what I wanted in a laptop, plus if I am going to develop games I need to review a lot to get my own ideas."

Well there it is less then an hour at college and I have a friend. After I finished unpacking Tony and I went to get our schedules and check out the campus. Since he was there a day before me he already met a few people and introduced them to me. One person would be the reason that I am here. Her name was Crystal, a beautiful blond with amazing blue eyes. She was a creative writing student and came out from the east coast to this school. The thing that intrigued me was just the way she looked at me and smiled. Every moment we were together was as if we were the last people on earth. She really liked me, and I had feelings for her like I never had before in my life. In fact I was always shy around girls and never had a girlfriend. So I hope I don't act like a dork and ruin this……or did I already by just staring at her.

Months went by and Crystal and I became close…..friends. Although I wanted more I didn't know if she felt the same way. We would walk at night together, go and get coffee or just sit around and talk. Then one night she told me something I didn't want to here.

"I met the most incredible guy today. I met him at the coffee shop; he's a poet and song writer. Nothing is more sexy then a guy in touch with his feelings." She was so happy looking. "We are going out tonight, and I had to tell someone. Brian I think this guy is someone I could really be with. He's is tall, smart and I melt when he looks at me."

I know the feeling; this is how I feel about you. How could she do this to me? She has to know how I feel. I could actually feel my heart breaking, I could feel my eyes tearing up, but I wouldn't let her see me cry. "I am happy for you….but I got to go." I had to get out of there; I couldn't stand being close to her.

"Brian! Wait, what's wrong? Come back please and talk to me." Crystal yelled as I walked away.

I got back to my dorm and Tony wasn't there. I think he had a math class so I knew I'd be alone for a while. I just laid there numb, wanting to cry but couldn't. Why should I be upset, it's not like she was my girlfriend. I was deep in thought about this when a voice came to me.

"Go see who he is. That's your woman don't let him take her from you."

I looked around to see who said it and no one was there. I got up and looked outside the door into the hall but it was empty. When I closed the door the voice reappeared.

"Did you forget about me?" I looked behind me and there he stood. I never knew who he was, just a figments of my own imagination. But there he stood as many times before. He stood at a slight slant and had a menacing look to him. "Come on now when will you become a man and fight for what's yours. I have tried to help and all you have done is ignore me. Why you little twit, why do you ignore me?"

"Who are you and what do you want? And why do you people keep coming to me?" It took all I could to get those words out.

"Well let's put it this way. Us people look after you and always have. Face it, you're a lil' wimp. You never will be anything, unless you listen to us. Everything you have gotten in life is cuz of us. So now we have to control this for you. You want her right?"

"Yes"

"Well then let's go see this guy and tell him to back off."

The door opened and Tony walked in. "I forgot my damn calculator." is all he said as he walked through our uninvited guest. "Dude its cold in here tonight. Turn up the heat some ok." And he walked out.

"What are you, a ghost?"

"I have been described as many of things," he said with a laugh,"now let's go."

Well maybe he is a guardian angel. Who knows, but as I walked across the quad to the street, no one else noticed he was there. He simply let them walk through him. Some people even shivered as we strolled past, like a cold blast of air hit them on a hot summer's eve. In fact as I stopped for traffic before crossing a street he kept going and stopped in the middle of traffic laughing calling me names. Just letting cars pass through him

We got to the coffee house and there stood a tall, rather good looking guy. A big smile on his face, as if he knows he stole my girl. He was taller then me and in better shape but my friend wouldn't let me turn back.

"Are you going to be a puss forever? Go tell him to forget about our woman."

"Our woman.....what do you mean?"

"Just get your scrawny ass over there and tell him to back off. Grow some balls boy. You can't be a lil' mama's boy forever."

So I started walking over to the counter. My throat was going dry, and my hands were sweating. I was getting hot but had an eerie cold spot on my back as if it was a hand pushing me. I walked slowly up close to the guy nervously, very intimidated. He looked at me and asked if he could help me.

"I don't want you to see Crystal." I said under my breath.

"Excuse me?"

"Can I get a cup of coffee?" I said louder. He turned to get it for me.

"You are a wimp. Maybe you should go back to your room and cry like a little school girl. You don't deserve my services." said a voice in my ear, "be a man or I will be one for you."

"I can't," I whispered.

"Fine, I will take care of him."

I looked up and saw Crystal's new guy coming towards me with a to-go cup. All of a sudden a coffee pot exploded, and then another. Shards of glass were flying around but not falling to the ground. People were screaming and running for cover as I stood there and watched a large piece of glass cut across the coffee guy's throat. He dropped the cup and grabbed his throat as glass started to find its target. His body was getting hit with glass and blood started to run down his recently white tee shirt. As I began to get scared a piece of large piece of glass exited through his stomach and he dropped to the floor. Then as if someone just through up a stop sign all the glass fell to the ground and the temperature dropped 10 degrees. An evil laugh then appeared.....it was coming out of my mouth.

I ran out the door like most of the customers already have, ready to have a nervous breakdown. I finally stopped running when I got to the quad, and collapsed. Filled with emotions I didn't know what to do. I could hear sirens in the background. I knew I wasn't in trouble but I also couldn't explain what happened.

"You liked that, huh? Well now it's your girlfriends turn. She will now be yours and my deed will be done."

"What deed? What do you want from me?" I said with pain in my voice

"I want you to listen, I want you to obey. You will obey me."

As if I got pulled up by strings my body lifted to my feet. I didn't even have control over my body and where did he go? I went up to my room and looked out the window and instead of seeing my own reflection I saw evil. I saw a grayish scarred face with an evil smile. Red glowing eyes looked back at me, but was that me? I ran out of the room to the bathroom and threw up, barely making the toilet. Then I looked up from the toilet and felt nothing. No pain, no pity, and no regret. Inside my head I heard the evil laugh again. I grinned as I got up to find Crystal.

I walked numbly to her room and entered without knocking. She was standing in front of a mirror putting on make up. She was in a tight black dress and high heels. It looked like she spent a lot of time doing her hair, because I was use to seeing it in a ponytail.

"My god Brian you scared me. I heard a lot of sirens do you know what happened?"

"Your boyfriend got killed. Guess you can go out with me tonight."

"What? How do you know this? Brian that is the cruelest joke you can play, so stop."

"I am not playing. He is dead. The twit is dead, I was there. I watched him die. Now you and I can be together without him interfering." I know I said these things but I don't know how or why. It's like someone took over my body. I am just a puppet doing what ever this thing wants me to do.

"Brian go! GET OUT. I DON'T LIKE WHATS GOING ON. LEAVE NOW," Crystal said crying and I knew she was scared. It kind of excited me.

I slammed the door shut and locked it. Then I turned to her, and in a voice that only I have heard before I told her to shut up.

"I did this for you, and for me, for us. We were meant to be together. And you had to go play around on me. Didn't you know you were mine and only mine? Now tell me my sweet how much do you love me?"

She looked at me and told me the most hurtful words I ever heard. "I don't love you. We are friends, Brian that's all. I am sorry if you felt different."

Rage poured over me and a burning on my back. My eyes felt like they would bust out of my head. My hands clinched tighter then ever before.

"Well I guess I have to take what I want….and I want you"

I grabbed her by the hair and threw her on the bed. She tried to get up and I pushed her back down. I looked at her and she screamed. All I did was laugh and slap her. Lowering my head to hers grasping her hair to control her head I stuck my tongue in her mouth. It was good….soft and wet. Then there was knocking on the door. I knew it was Tony, I could hear him yelling for her. Then the door flew open and he ran towards me. I stuck my hand up and imbedded it into his chest grabbing onto his heart. I ripped it out of him and watched him fall.

Then turning my attention back to Crystal, I started grabbing her breast and rubbing them as I tried again to kiss her. Her crying was getting annoying and I slapped her so hard blood started coming out of her ear. I reached down under her dress and tore her underwear off. She didn't move, maybe she was more willing now. I unzipped my pants and pulled myself out as a sharp pain came to my head. I was hit....I was knocked out cold.

The next thing I knew I awoke strapped down to a gurney and police all around me. I couldn't believe everything that happened was real. But it was......I killed my best friend at college, a person I didn't know, and tried to rape the girl I loved. Why? I am not like that.....or am I? As the ambulance doors shut and started moving I could see my unwilling counterpart in the glass. He smiled and I heard him talk again.

"See I got you what you wanted. Remember it when you want more." He said that he can control everything around me, but why me?

The court declared me to be incompetent to stand trial for reason of insanity. Now I am stuck in this hospital for life. No family, no friends, no one except my demon friend. And still no one hears what I do or sees what I see.

2
THEIR HOUSE

It was a dream of ours to have an old country house. And in North Carolina they were plentiful, beautiful 200 year old plantation houses. My wife and I were glad when we finally found an old farm house we liked, and about a quarter of the going cost. We couldn't pass up this deal. Mostly when you find a cheap house it's because it's in need of repair. This house was in perfect condition and only minimal work done, mostly cleaning.

The house built in the early 1800's has been abandoned for a few years. No one knows why the family that lived there just packed up and moved. Across the field stood a barn which needed either to be torn down or to be fixed. I personally was afraid to walk into the building for fear it would crash on top of me. But I had to venture in to see if there was anything in there besides cobwebs and dirt. Our oldest son Nathan came with me to check it out. What we found would change our lives.

I am John Weerey and around 10 years ago I married a wonderful woman Sarah. After two years of marriage we were blessed by Nathan and three years after that the twins. Michael and Michaela were quite a surprise to us, but a miracle altogether. After five years in a small three bedroom home we had to find something large. I now have to drive an hour to work in the morning but its well worth coming home. And the best thing is we made money selling our house and our payments on the new house are way lower then before. So how could we lose?

The first Sunday after we moved in Nathan wanted to explore the barn. Well to be honest I wanted to know if it was in good enough shape to be use as a garage and for storage. So I agreed and informed Sarah of our exploration at hand.

Nathan took the lead by running up to the door but suddenly stopped and waited for me to enter with him. He reached up and took hold of my hand, I knew he was scared. As I looked around, I didn't like what I saw. Animal dropping spread about as well as fallen wood from the barn. The first thing I thought of is to have it bulldozed and have a new pole barn put up in its place. So we ventured on and in the back corner I could see where the dirt floor looked like it was burnt. I told Nathan to go back inside and I would be there shortly, he followed my directions and ran back in the house.

As I walked to the back of the barn I could defiantly smell that something was burnt back there. There was no one for at least 3 miles in any direction so vandals were probably out of the question. When I came to a corner where the smell was the strongest I found an old chest……something like a hope chest. It looked really old and that it was in a fire. So I drag it out into the sunlight to take a better look.

Sarah walked out of the house to see what kind of treasure I have found. I looked over the lock which looked like it had been damaged, seeing if I could pry it open. There had to be something in there because the weight of the box.

"What did you find?" asked Sarah.

"Well you can see it, you know as much as I do. I found it in the back of the barn."

"Well what's inside of it"

I just rolled my eyes back. Sometimes I swear that she was as stupid as road kill but she did hold a master's degree in literary art. Making sure I wouldn't say anything stupid which might end up with me sleeping on the couch for a week.

"I don't really know, I have to get a pry bar to break open the lock"

"Why don't you use the key?"

There are my eyes rolling again,"I don't have it"

"Yes you do, it's on a chain on the other handle."

Ok so she got this one, but when she thought her gay brother's girlfriend was really a woman…..I got that one.

"Well let's see if it will open." I said while placing the key in the lock. CLICK…It was unlocked. The wood creaked when I lifted the top, the hinges totally rusted. Inside was a book, a diary.

Also was a picture of a man and a woman in front of our house. The picture was old and yellowing from age. At the bottom was a note…..

"We built this house, we lived here, and we raised our children here. The war has taken our children without return. The war has taken our crops with out return. The wars has taken us ….we will return"

Wow I thought, a very heart felt message and probably from the days of the civil war. What a collectible and it all ties in with the house. I was ecstatic.

"Hun lets bring this all into the house and find homes for them. I think this picture would look great upon the mantle."

She agreed and we brought the items inside. I dug through a box and found a frame we were not using and I placed the picture and note inside it. Sarah in the meantime was already looking through the diary. I put the picture upon the mantle and stood back like I painted a masterpiece, but I just wanted to take in the picture with the fireplace. It did bring a piece of the past into the old house.

"Did you know that the people that built this house also had a large plantation in the southern half of the state? And the last entry in here says the rebels were coming and they had to hide in the root cellar. Do we have a root cellar?"

"I haven't found one as of yet but maybe I will have to look for one," I told her.

After dinner the kids went into the entrance way to watch a movie as Sarah and I decided to relax and sit in the parlor with a book. Her with her romantic novel and mine on how to repair old plaster we sat there with out talking. The sound of the TV in the adjacent room was the only noise in the house. Although it was just my wife and I sitting there I felt like I was being watched. I'd look around to see if one of the kids came in the room and did that "I want something stare" but no one was there. It must have been my imagination.

Well we retired to the bedroom at around 10 and the kids have been asleep for at least two hours and all I thought was I could use a good night sleep. Just after I started to fall into a deep sleep I heard a yell from the twin's room. I jumped out of bed to see what was wrong. Because it's been along time since a child woke up in the middle of the night. Michaela was hiding under her covers crying and yelling for us.

"What's wrong sweetie; did you have a bad dream?"

"No, the old woman woke me up and wanted me to go with her."

"What old woman?"

"The old woman with the man, they said I had to go."

Feeling this is a dream, I assured her that there was no woman and she should go back to sleep. Behind me, my wife stood with a loving smile and helped tuck our girl back into bed. We even left a small light on for her.

We then went back to bed without a sound and returned to our sleep.

The next morning was a stressful one. For some reason, my alarm did not go off and I was going to be late for work. Luckily it was summer vacation or the kids would be running around as much as I was. But I made it out only about 10 minutes late and figured I could make it up on the road. I work for a cement contractor and really love my job. When I was made company manager I really stepped up my game. Never late, never absent in 4 years. I respected my workers as I hope they did me and they became like a second family to me.

Around mid day I was going over some invoices when I received a call from my wife telling me that the lights went out. Well it's a house that hasn't been used in years so that was bound to happen. I told her where the fuse box was and how to change the fuse. Then I told her if she had any trouble leave it and I would fix it when I got home. Being daytime we didn't really need the lights.

When I got home the power was on, but I was in fear of seeing my wife with an unexpected perm. She met me at the door with a surprised look on her face, to the point where I thought she was going to wet herself right there.

"I want out of this house, there is something creepy here."

"Come on, there is nothing wrong it's just that you were home alone with the kids for the first time."

She put her head down and walked back inside. She kept saying she was told to get out by someone but no one was around. She was just disgusted with me for not believing her and went up to bed early. It's just being in a new house that's all. But that night made me believe her.

Around 3 in the morning I was awoke by a loud noise. My first thought is one of the kids fell out of bed. When I got to the twins room Michael wasn't there, I called for Sarah and we started searching for him. When I got in the kitchen I looked out the window and saw him walking towards an old tree. The thing that puzzled me was he held his hand up like he was holding somebody's hand. I opened the door and yelled for him with no response. I then ran out to get him, maybe he was sleepwalking.

When I got to him he looked at me and said I scared off his friend and his wife. Ok now this is starting to get weird. I told him he was dreaming and he had to go to bed. Sarah finally caught up to us and then took him back inside. I saw something I wanted to look at by the tree. As I walked over I saw the old root cellar. It was partially buried and hasn't been used for a long time. I thought it would be better to investigate it the next day and went back to bed. But sleep wasn't in the cards.

As I walked in past the parlor I smelled something burning, and at the same time I heard my wife scream. I ran upstairs to finally see what my family has been seeing. It was the old couple from the picture we found.

"This is our house and you can't make us leave," said the old man. Needless to say all I thought about was getting the hell out of there.

We grabbed the kids and headed down the stairs. I stopped briefly in the parlor and the fire place was burning. And I looked to the picture and it too was burning. I ran to catch up with the family and help pile the kids in the car. Then the lights and horn started going off and the key wasn't even in the ignition. The kids then ran out of the car. Why was Michael walking towards the old root cellar.......maybe the old couple is still there? I told Sarah to take the kids to the barn and I grabbed an old shovel and started to unbury the cellar.

The sound of unearthly screams rang out through the night. Knowing that it was not my family I kept digging. The wind started to blow and a chill came into the air but I had to see. I uncovered one door and tried to open it. At that moment the old man got right in my face telling me to leave them alone. The sudden shock of him being there startled me and I lost my balance and fell through the rotted door. After landing I saw two skeletons sitting on the ground, and looked around to see that the walls were burnt and had a feeling that they died in the fire.

I prayed to set there souls free and let them be released of this curse that held them earth bound. After the second recital of the Lord's Prayer a whoosh of cold air and a blood curdling scream went past me. Then a sudden feeling of peace and tranquility fell upon me. I reached up and pulled myself out of the cellar and ran back to my family. Feeling our ordeal was over we went back into the house. No burning smell, and the picture was normal, not even a scorch mark.

We placed the picture, note, and diary back in the box and left it in the cellar. In the years to come, we never had a problem again. Maybe the old couple is finally free too.

3
THE ACCIDENT

My name is Brett, and I am lucky to be alive. I am laying here in this hospital room just coming out of a coma after 3 weeks. My girl friend Barb never left my side; she lost her job and put her life on hold for me. After I woke up I told her of the events leading up to me being here, as strange as they may be. It must have been a sign from my family.

See a few weeks ago I was out drinking with a few guys from work. Well it was coming up on 9 and I had plans with Barb so I scooted out of there. Knowing I shouldn't drive, I still didn't want to be late so I got in my car and started off down the street. I have made it home safely may times after drinking so what would make this night any different. The rain should have been my warning sign.

Then it happened, I didn't see the red light. A truck came through the intersection and hit me broad side. I sat there motionless until I passed out.

When my eyes opened I saw my grandparents, they passed away many years ago. Does this mean I am dead too. I feel no pain and I am overwhelmed by tranquility. What about Barb? What will happen to her?

"Brett, get up son." said my grandfather, "We need to talk."

"Pops you died when I was 15. Am I dead or is this a dream?"

"As I said we need to talk. There were many of things I never was able to say to you. Now I have a chance."

Still confused about what happened I sat up and listened to him.

"Things have to change, your life has changed. Now it's up to you to make a decision."

He lowered his hand and helped me to my feet. We started walking towards a house, their old house. How can this be, it was torn down 3 years ago. Man I got to quit drinking. I have wrecked my car, I missed my date with Barb, and now I am thinking that I'm going to my grandparent's house. I am in bad shape.

"Come in honey, I will get some iced tea," said my grandmother.

"Yes come in and sit. It's been a long time since you have been here, relax. Now your live is going good right? So why are you not trying to make it worth it? I mean you have a woman who loves you, a good job, and you just bought a new condo. What were you planning next?"

"I don't know Pop. I guess have Barb move in."

My grandmother walked in carrying a tray of tea and glasses. "Oh my! Living together, that won't do. If you love her take her as your wife."

"I don't know if I am ready for marriage. I mean I love her but …."

"Son, if you love her then marry her! Let your heart decide. Does your heart hurt when you are not around her? Like now?"

At that moment I felt an incredible pain in my chest. I bent over grasping for my heart. It felt like an intense shock, and the pain started to fade. Just as I was about to finally be relieved of the pain and catch my breath it happened again. I fell forward……

"Son, you have to stay here until we get your life straight. I want you to go home, but now is not the time."

What does he mean? Now, I am more confused then before. Even to make things worst I notice that I have what looks to be pin holes over on my left hand. And blood started to drip, then like magic it disappeared. Ok no more Jack, beer still will be fine.

"Ok Brett first of all, you're a drunk."

"I am not," I replied loudly. "Just because I got out in drink does not mean I'm a drunk"

"No son, you are a drunk. You drink every day until your drunk, and then you drink more. Can you explain why?"

I looked at him blankly. He hasn't been around for so many years and he knows nothing about me. How can he judge, he is dead.

"Ok this is what you have to do," Pop said as he leaned back. "You must quit and you must be with your true love. Would that be Barb?"

Barb and I have been together for around 2 years, and yes I love her. She has been there for me always. So I guess she's my love. "Yes, I guess so."

"And you want to grow old with her, like your grandmother and I have right."

"Yes"

"Then you must go to her. Be with her, and make a better life for yourself."

My grandmother walked towards me. Her smile always made me feel like nothing could ever hurt me. The gleam in her eyes was as bright as it was when I was a child. After all these years I still miss them, and still need them.

"Here, give her this," my grandmother said as she held out her hand. There sitting on her palm was a ring, a diamond ring. "This is the ring your grandfather gave me when he asked me to marry him. It's only fitting that you do the same."

I reached out and took the ring in my hands. Looking at it, and then looking at my grandmother's smile. How could I say no?

"Its time son," said my grandfather. "Remember this moment. And always know we are with you. No matter what family is always with you"

At that moment I felt a pull. Then another and I started to feel light headed. Things began to spin. I dropped to my knees. What was happening? When I looked up I saw my grandparents smiling at me, and they were wishing me well. I couldn't breath, and it felt like I was on an out of control merry-go-round. I tried my hardest to say good bye but nothing would come out.

In a flash I was drawn out of their house and across a field. I was above the ground watching everything fly by me so quickly it was a blur. I started to fade in and out of conciseness. Then everything went white…….no sound, no color, nothing. I felt weightless, just floating motionless. For the first time today I didn't worry about any thing, I didn't feel any pain, nothing. Where am I?

I floated there for what seemed to be an hour then in the distance I saw Barb. She was crying, sitting there. I tried to call to her but nothing came out. Seeing her cry broke my heart. I never wanted her to feel pain. Especially pain I created. She meant more to me then life itself. I wished I could be with her at that moment.

As I watched her I began to feel her pain, and when that happened the white light became dark. I didn't feel weightless any more. In fact I felt a lot of pain. I couldn't move my left leg and my head was pounding. I opened my eyes to see barb sitting there crying. As she looked over to me she smiled and stood up.

"Brett, you're awake. Oh thank you God. I thought I lost you," she said now crying for a different reason.

"I love you Barb….."

"I love you too."

At that moment as she bent down to kiss me I felt something in my hand. I opened up my hand to see what it was. It was my grandmother's ring, just like it was in the dream. But how, and was it a dream?

"Barb, I don't know where to begin. I'm sorry and I love you. Will you marry me?"

"Yes Brett, yes, but ….where did that come from?"

I didn't know at the time but I died. They shocked me to get a heart beat again. And I was in a coma for weeks. IV's placed in my left hand were removed and placed back in and my hand was bruised badly. My right hand, the one the ring was in, was usually held by Barb day and night. So how did the ring get there? Who cares?

I slid the ring onto Barbs left ring finger and once again I felt that tranquility. This time it was because of her, not something I couldn't explain. Knowing that I would be ok I did have to change my life. Just like my grandparents I wanted to spend the rest of my life with Barb. And I knew she felt the same way.

4
The sleep over

When we were teenagers, we did some real stupid things. But one stands out in my mind because it still haunts me today. It all happened at a sleep over when I was fifteen. My name is Leslie and I am twenty nine now, divorced with a two year old. The events that happened back in high school continue today and its part of my life now and there is nothing I can do about it.

Years ago, my friend Tina had a sleep over with some other girls from the neighborhood. Its not like we never have done it before, usually someone was having a get together once a week. That night was different though. Yes we did the scary movie and popcorn thing; also bash boys which we did the most. But Tina had a just got an Ouija board. I never believed in them or in ghost. But I went along with it any way.

After watching a couple slasher movies our heart rate was already over two million and Tina brought out the board.

"This will be fun; maybe we can contact Kurt Corbain." said Tina in a deep voice. "Maybe contact the devil himself…."

"Come on you know this isn't real, it's just a game in the toy isle. Ghosts aren't real and you cannot contact the dead. Once you are dead that's it your dead. Never to be heard from again. We have been friends for years, and this is probably the stupidest thing you ever suggested."

"Ohhhhh, it sounds like Leslie is scared. Maybe she doesn't want to play and find out the secrets to the universe," said Tina.

"How can you be scared it's a toy? That's all it is, nothing more."

"Then you can go first," said Beth.

Tina and I were great friends and always have been. She is really smart and always cared for others. She had natural brown curly hair and wore glasses. I myself always considered myself as average. Nothing really to speak of just normal. I have dark hair, brown eyes, average height and a little chubby. No I am not fat just didn't exercise much. Now Beth on the other hand, what she lacked in brains she made up for in looks. Beth was a very pretty girl and always got attention. Long blond hair and blue eyes, and a body of a supermodel, Beth had it all. I might sound jealous but I know that I was a better person. The thing that really bugged me was that she was so stuck on herself.

"Beth do you ever have nothing to say?" I questioned her and I believed it was a good one.

"Well I have nothing to say about your hair, you know if you don't have anything good to say."

Gawd I would love to suffocate her with her pillow. "Just let's play this stupid game ok."

Tina set everything up as Beth brushed her hair and I picked up spilt popcorn. Like Beth was going to help, she might break a nail. I just don't know why I didn't like her so much, maybe because she just cared for herself. She was the most selfish person I knew. But she was popular; hence I was with the in crowd.

"Ok I will go first, what you do is hold on to this thing and asks questions." Tina never read instructions just did things. Most of the time she was right on the ball, and I did say most times.

After a series of questions nothing really happened. I think the biggest thing was a breeze created by me yawning. Well it was eleven thirty and I was getting tired.

I went back over by the bed to let Beth have more room as she and Tina kept trying to contact Kurt. Then Beth took control trying to find out if there was anyone around us. Maybe she was trying to contact Oz to ask for a brain.

"This is boring, I'm going to go to sleep," Beth said with an attitude.

She walked into the bathroom to prep for bed. Like you need to look beautiful before you went to sleep. I threw my hair back into a loose ponytail and lay down in the bed with Tina. That way the princess would have the other bed to herself.

When I first looked at the clock it was twelve fifteen. Then again at twelve thirty, I just couldn't fall asleep. Then I heard a scraping, like something being grabbed and slide against cardboard. I looked down to the floor and I saw the planchette move. That's the pointer for the Ouija board. I crawled out of bed to check out why it was moving. Beth and Tina were sleep so I knew they weren't doing it.

I got to the board and it spelled out a word….."Do". The hair on the back of my neck was standing straight up as it spelled out the words "want her". The last word scared me badily. The word "dead" was spelled out.

"Who?" I asked the board. Now I was starting to believe.

Then the pointer started to move again and went to the letter "b". "Beth?" I asked. And it went to "yes on the board.

"No, I may not like her so much but I don't wish her dead."

It took awhile but "nobody said good bye" was spelled out. Geez I haven't talked to a toy since I was eight. Now I am getting ragged on for not saying good bye to a game. I started to think I was dreaming then the pointer started moving. It said we all were in danger, and someone will die. I got sick of it and picked the board up and put it back into the box then proceeded to go back to bed.

Not even five minutes later I smelled smoke. I looked over to the box and smoke was pouring through the cracks. I woke up Tina and showed her the smoke; she naturally screamed waking up sleeping beauty. We all stared into the moonlit room watching smoke seep through the box.

"This is nuts," said Beth as she went for the box. As she got to it the closet door flew open causing Tina to scream once again. It startled Beth but she still went to open the box. As she did a great cloud of smoke came out, at least there was no fire.

After the box was opened the smoke stopped. She pulled the board out and opened it up and there was something burned on the board. Tina reached over to turn on the light and we got out of bed to check on what it said.

We all looked down and Beth's name was burned plain as day into the board.

"Ok….I know this is a joke, now who did it? Was it you Leslie? I bet it was because you're jealous of me. You're not as pretty as me and I bet you never had a boyfriend."

It was true but I was still getting really mad. How dare her to say such cruel things.

"Tina, you really have to get better friends. This little joke she's playing is sick." Beth ranted as she walked back over to the bed.

"I didn't do anything Tina." I told her softly.

At that moment Beth fell to the floor like she got knocked down. Coldness came into the room and the lights flickered. Beth started yelling for me to get off of her but I was standing five feet away. Tina held on to my arm as Beth fought her invisible attacker. She turned her head and saw both of us standing there in fright now knowing that I wasn't fighting her and she screamed.

Tina's dad entered the room to see what all the screaming was about and saw Beth on the floor. He then proceeded to walk over there to help her up and when he got there he was hit and thrown across the room. Then a deep voice was heard. It sounded so scary and not human.

"No one said good bye to me. Now maybe you will start showing me respect."

At that moment Beth was lifted up to her feet and as if she was a puppet she started walking to the door. You could see the tears running down her face. She exited the room and made her way down the stairs.

We ran after her, almost tripping over each other. We yelled for her to stop as she opened the front door. She turned and looked at us mouthing the word help. Still crying she started to run. Faster then we ever have seen her move before. And as she ran down the block the street lights all dimmed as she came near them.

We followed her but couldn't keep up. She had like superhuman speed. And she was dressed like us, which was a night shirt and no shoes on. How could she run so quickly? Then she made a turn and she was out of sight. We ran back to Tina's house as her dad was starting to pull out of the driveway. As we jumped in the car her dad asked what the hell was going on. We explained but I don't think he believed us.

As we drove to find Beth we tried to explain everything and he just blew it off. We drove around for a while then we found her. She looked right as us as she stood next to a busy street. The bars were just closing up so there was more traffic then most areas at this time of night. A menacing look came across Beth's face and she grinned at us. Then she turned and ran into traffic. She got hit and was thrown about fifty feet into the street.

We got out of the car and ran to her. She was dead, but she still had a grin on her face.

After the police and ambulance started to leave we got back in the car and headed back to Tina's house. The car ride back was quiet and sorrowful. We were almost home and "who's next?' came out of the car speakers. The radio wasn't even on. Tina and I looked at each other and started crying immediately.

We ran inside to the Ouija board and said goodbye. The lights then began to return to its original brightness and the room warmed up again. Tina and I looked at each other and began to cry over the nights events.

The next morning was one full of dread and confusion. When we woke both of us prayed that it was all a dream and Beth was still asleep in the other bed. But she wasn't.

I got up and started to get a pair of shorts on when I notice on the Ouija board more words appeared. "Good night" was burned into the board; a reminder of the night was shared. We grabbed the board and threw it into the box, taking it out of the house, hoping that the garbage man would dispose of all of its evil.

Years have passed and Tina and I are still friends. Although we are both divorced and bounce from job to job we blame it all on that board. We will never forget that night, and the hair stands on the back of neck every time we walk into the game isle. It's not really a game, it's not a toy. It's a horror that will never go away.

5

The doll

It's a beautiful day and we are out antiquing. Just Trinie and me, Trinie is my daughter. After my husband became sheriff of this little town and we moved here I have been looking for something to do. Kevin wanted to get into a small town and I wanted to stay in the city. I'm not really into rural living; the population out here is only five hundred people. So buying antiques became a big hobby for me. Out here the prices are cheaper and the items are in better condition.

We moved out here after Kevin's sister died. She got herself in with the wrong crowd and was killed in a drive by shooting. We were her guardians since his parents passed away a few years ago and I guess she rebelled against us because she couldn't accept the fact her parents were dead. We tried everything, not even counseling helped.

Trinie is a two years old now and getting into everything. She talks a lot for a little one and she's very demanding. The only bad thing is she explores so much, and has to touch everything around her. So I have to watch her well or go broke in these stores.

"Come on Trinie; let's go see if they got anything new in."

I picked her up out of the car seat and carried her in. This particular antique store is probably my least favorite. I always get a creepy feeling in here; I don't know what it is. Maybe it's the musky smell or just some of the really odd items here. Some might be even satanic, well maybe.

As I was looking at a tea set from the eighteen hundreds, Trinie saw an old porcelain doll. I had to have the tea set and it was only forty dollars. It's hard to find a silver tea set for forty bucks back in the city. It was tarnished badly but I can clean it up. And when my mom comes to visit she will love it as much as I do.

"Mama Dolly, I want dolly," said Trinie.

I walked over and looked at the price. 1 dollar fifty, well ok if that will keep her occupied for now. I walked over to the counter to pay.

"Hello Mrs. Wilkinson, you find everything ok?" said the old man behind the counter.

"Yes sir and I want that tea set along with this doll."

"Are you sure you want this doll. I've had it for years, and no one has even asked about it. In fact I have gotten many of complaints about it. Some even say that it watches them. Now are you sure you want it."

Well Trine really wants it. And the face is a bit creepy. Can you tell me where it was made and how old it is?"

"It was made in Europe some where over a hundred years ago." The old man continued,"the person that sold it to me was a strange one. She was in her sixties and she traded it to me for a pack of matches. Do you believe that, matches? She said that it was her great aunts when she was a child. But the child died of fever, at a very young age. And ever since then the doll possesses an evil that no priest was ever able to get rid of. So I am going to suggest that you don't by it."

I took the old mans advice and let him put it back as he brought up the tea set. I watched him as he wrapped it up and bagged it. Afterwards I walked out with my tea set and Trinie still in my now numb arm. When we got back to the car I put the bag in the trunk and Trinie in her car seat.

Oddly to me Trinie was not upset with putting the doll back. Usually I would have to listen to an hour of whining when she doesn't get what she wants.

After we got home I started to clean up the silver. When I reached to get the tea pot out of the bag, I found a big surprise. The doll was in there. How did it get in the bag, I saw the old man put it back on the shelf. But here it is right in my hand now. Did Trinie grab it when we were walking out?

"Trinie? Did you take this doll off the shelf at the store?" She looked at me blankly. "Well its going back, I didn't pay for it. Mommy is really upset with you honey."

I grabbed the phonebook to look up the stores number so I could call and apologize straight off. After dialing the number the phone rang at least ten times, what don't they have voice mail. Damn small town living. They must be closed so I will wait till morning. Anyway I have to start dinner Kevin will be home soon.

I put Trinie down for a nap and started dinner. Nothing too fancy just some pork chops and potatoes. As I was peeling the potatoes Kevin walked in. After a quick peck on the lips he proceeded to tell me about his day. Compared to my day his day was a breeze. I found a runaway dog and got a ticket for going to slow on the highway.

He sat down with a soda at the kitchen table and noticed the tea set. Still talking about the old man he ticketed he started to look at the pot.

"I see you found something you liked today."

"Yeah, isn't it great?" I replied. "It was really cheap, almost a steal. Speaking of which, do you know what your daughter did today. She stole a doll in the antique store. I am so embarrassed."

"Well she's a kid that happens just explain what happened and all should be fine."

"I tried to call but they must have been closed. I am going to try in the morning. Then I have to go back into town to return them."

"Welcome to parenthood baby."

He gave me a little kiss on the cheek and walked out of the room. I finished cooking dinner and called for him. Then I called again, still no answer. So I went into the living room to see what was keeping Kevin from dinner.

He was just staring at the doll. Both looked sad, I don't know how but the doll looked sad. I could even see a tear running down Kevin's face. The only time I ever saw him cry is when his sister died.

"Honey, what's wrong?"

"I don't know I picked up the doll and I was hit with emotion. I just remembered every bad thing in my life, all at once."

He put the doll down and I followed him into the kitchen. There wasn't much talking during dinner; Kevin really was not like himself at all. He didn't even eat that much.

After dinner he did help clear the table and as I started the water I heard Trinie in the living room. I walked in to see if it was her and it was. She must have climbed out of her crib and walked out here.

"Honey, you know you're not supposed to get out of your crib without mommy or daddy."

"Dolly got me. She woke me up and told me to come here."

"A doll can't talk, and you know that. Now let's get you some dinner."

"Bye-bye dolly, see you after I eat," Trinie said sweetly.

Kevin already started dishes when we got back in the kitchen. And the baby said hi right away and gave daddy a big kiss. Then I sat her in her high chair and cut some food up for her. Half way through dishes we heard a crash in the other room Kevin got out there first. And the clock on the mantle had fallen and broke apart.

"Never had a problem like that before, wonder how it fell," said Kevin.

We cleaned up the mess and I glanced over to the table with the doll on it and it looked like the doll was grinning. Defiantly it had a different expression on its face. But how, it's a doll. I thought it must be my imagination, so I continued to clean up the clock.

That whole evening was strange. Trinie was talking to the doll, even had a full conversation. Nothing weird there just the baby playing, but both Kevin and I heard voices from no where and I swear I saw someone walk through the kitchen. I think the old man's story made me a little scared. I really didn't want the doll in the house after that but here we are.

After the baby was in bed for about an hour Kevin and I headed up to bed too. I checked on Trinie and to my astonishment the doll was in her crib with her. But how did it get there, we left it down stairs. I removed it from her bed and placed it in the hallway on a table. As I walked towards the bedroom door, it slammed in my face. I yelled at Kevin for shutting the door and he came out of the bathroom across the hall. I had blood dripping out of my nose and what confused me more was how did the door shut on me.

Kevin insisted that the door must have been closed and I was preoccupied by other things and didn't notice it. I got the bleeding to stop and still I knew what happened but getting him to believe that is a different story. While I was cleaning up I heard a loud bang from our room. I ran in the room to see Kevin flat on his back.

"I swear I just got pushed out of bed. But no one is here, what the hell is going on?"

I stopped in my tracks to go check on the baby. As I ran pass the hallway table I noticed the doll was not there. I got to her room and the doll was back in her bed with her. I grabbed the doll and opened the window. As hard as I could I threw the doll out the window and it landed in the front yard. As far as I was concerned it could stay there.

We went to bed and all was well for a while, until what sounded like the front door slamming. Not once but three or four times. Kevin grabbed his gun, thinking it was a prowler. He went down stairs and I went to get the baby. As I picked Trinie up I heard a gunshot. I knew it was stupid to go down stairs but I did anyway. And at the base of the stairs was Kevin, out cold.

The door was still slamming shut over and over. I was afraid to even see if Kevin was alive I ran back upstairs and hid in our bedroom. By this time the baby was crying loudly and I couldn't calm her down in the state I was in, then something started banging on the door. Like someone was trying to break it down I yelled for who ever was there to go away. And it stopped.

Finally it was all over, who ever or whatever it was went away.

All of a sudden the banging came back and the furniture in the room started to shake. Dresser drawers shot out as if blown out of a cannon. The pillows started to fly across the room. I didn't know what to do so I ran for the door, opened it and saw no one was there and ran for the baby's room.

We removed the lock on the door right after Trinie locked us out one day, so I was screwed. I could hear footsteps coming down the hall and looked for somewhere to hide. As I turned to the window I noticed that the doll wasn't where I threw it. I glanced towards the crib and saw the doll back in it. It is possessed; its evil and I brought it into my house.

I went to grab the doll to remove it once again from the house and a voice appeared out of no where.

"I want the girl, I want the girl." repeating over and over the same phrase.

"No you can't have her," I screamed.

I looked towards the doll again and it was frowning. No more grins or a blank look. It looked angry, mad.......or evil.

"If I can't have her, neither can you." said the voice again.

The crib started shaking, and the doll rose to its feet. The doll was moving, why me. I ran back towards the door but I couldn't open it. The side of the crib came off and flew at me hitting me across my back. I slid down the door in incredible pain. And while I did that I lost grip of Trinie. I tried to grab her but she went right towards the doll. I used all my might to lunge for her and basically tacking her as the door flew open and all I could hear was a gunshot.

It was Kevin, gun still smoking as he checked on us. He had blood coming out of his ear, I knew he was hurt. He asked if we were ok and all I could do is cry. He shot the head off the doll and a weight was lifted from me. The air seemed calm again, everything felt like it was suppose to. Except that the doll was still in the room.

Kevin picked it up and carried it outside and started to dig a hole. After it was deep enough I threw the doll in and he covered it back up. He held me tight after that as we stood there over the make shift grave of the doll. Then I noticed that Trinie wandered off. I turned in time to see her walk into the house and the door shut. An outline of a child appeared in the window upstairs.

We ran towards the house to save our daughter but when we got near the door there was an explosion. We were thrown back at least thirty feet and hit the ground with a thud. Glass and wood scattered throughout the yard. I looked up and through the tears I saw my Trinie holding hands with another girl. They were engulfed in flames, and then they were gone.

After the fire department put out the fire and searched for Trinie it became apparent that we would never see our daughter again. They never found her or the other girl, just a burnt porcelain doll.

6

LOVERS TO DEATH

It all started about two years ago, when I was happy. I was engaged to a very jealous man, but he treated me so well. I truly loved him and I miss him so much. Although he passed away the day we looked at our first house, he is still with me.......all the time. The day I am talking about we were in a car accident that took his life. I was still in the hospital during his funeral, and I never got to say goodbye. I still to this day regret that day.

As time went by I still think I see him everywhere. At work I would be at my desk and he would be standing there watching me with a smile on his face. I don't know if it was wishing he was here or just the memories. It started to get more and more regular, I started to wonder if I was going crazy. I saw him everywhere and could not stop thinking about him.

A few weeks later I saw a counselor about what was going on and basically just given some anti depressants and told to schedule another session. Now I am seeing him and I'm drugged. What a wonderful life, I am a drugged up loony, as my mother put it.

As time went on I didn't see Dan, my boyfriend, as much. Maybe I was starting to finally heal. I was feeling like my days were mine again and not consumed with guilt and wishful thinking. Work was getting better since I could concentrate more and a promotion was clearly in view.

Then one day while out with my friend Jackie, I met someone very interesting. His name was Mark, about two years older then me and very good looking. He had a certain confidence about him that was very attractive. The only flaw I saw was he had a little premature gray in his hair, but it made him look more dignified. He said he was an accountant for a very large firm downtown, so I figured he probably didn't live in a dingy hovel.

As he walked to get us drinks Jackie voiced, "Debbie it's been over two years don't you think its time you start dating again. Or should I make a reservation at the convent?"

"I don't know….he is a nice guy, but I just don't think I am ready yet." I tried to rationally come up with a reason not to start dating again but I couldn't think of one. To many drinks I guess, "Ok, ok, I will give him my number but we both know he won't call."

Well the next day rule was thrown out and he did call. We talked for hours and I hate to say it but Jackie was right. It was time and I could feel myself really liking talking to him. He told me about his work, what he likes to do, and his favorite movie. Believe me this was going to good. I started thinking what it would be like to actually start dating again, friends are one thing but this I don't think would be a friendship. Well in the long run it wouldn't.

As I was feeling more comfortable talking to him I made myself more relaxed in my apartment. Laying around on the couch, kicking my leg up laughing at his jokes, then he asked me out for dinner, which I replied yes to maybe a little too quick. At the same time I heard a crash in the bedroom. So I got up to check it out.

"Is everything ok?" asked Mark.

"Yeah, a picture fell off my dresser. The cat must have been up there and knocked it off," I replied. But there was something really bothering me. It was a picture of Dan and I that was taken a few days before our accident.

I told mark dinner would be great and he could pick me up at work. I gave him directions and disconnected so I could clean up the mess in my bedroom.

The next day I felt like a million bucks. My hair was perfect and on my lunch I bought a new pair of shoes for our date. The bad thing is the day dragged on forever. I never had a day go by so freaking slow. Five minutes before I was supposed to go my phone rang. It was an outside call so I figured it's probably Mark canceling. When I picked it up I heard nothing. I said hello a few times then hung up the phone. I didn't have time for childish pranks.

Mark was waiting for me outside when I walked out and he was so handsome standing there in what had to be a high end tailored suit. And our dinner date went as good as he looked, almost to perfect in my mind. He even walked me to my door and gave me a peck on my cheek, and told me he would call me tomorrow and walked away. Wow, my heart was beating so hard I was afraid he would hear it.

As I walked into my apartment it looked normal, but unusually cold. Maybe the air conditioner was stuck….no it wasn't even on and the thermometer said it was sixty-two degrees. That's a little weird for it being in the upper seventies that night. So I called the super and when he came up he couldn't find out what the problem was and said he would have to come back the next day.

Well since there wasn't anything I could do but open a few windows I disrobed and threw on a pair of comfy sweats and an oversized t-shirt. I passed on taking a shower till it warmed up a bit. I went in too take off my make up and wash my face and after I rinsed off the soap I looked in the mirror and I saw Dan staring at me. He looked madder then I ever seen him before. I turned around quickly to find that no one was there. Maybe it's just the guilt again. So I proceeded to bed hoping to have a good night sleep.

When I awoke the next morning I was drained.... I slept like crap. And I looked like it. I took a shower to wake up as the coffee was brewing. I was so peaceful; I can't remember even having a thought cross through my head. So after standing there for almost a half hour letting the hot water drown away my tiredness, I dried off and walked back into my bedroom where I found my entire closet thrown across my room. It was in shambles, clothes everywhere, and a shoe heel imbedded in the drywall. This I couldn't blame on the cat.

All I could do is break down and cry. Was I robbed, what did they take? I put on a robe and checked out the rest of the apartment and everything else was fine. And the chain was still in place on the front door. So how did they get in, and what did they want? I went back into the bedroom to take a better look. The shoe stuck in the wall was one of the shoes I bought the day before.

Well no time to clean it up now, I had to get ready for work. So I dug through the mess to find a suit I could wear. And got dressed and ran off to the train.

The whole day I could not concentrate on anything. The mess kept running through my head and I couldn't get it out. Finally I just left work to go home to clean and find answers. The train was overcrowded like always, but I couldn't help noticing a man staring at me. Then he started to walk towards me, for god's sake, now I got some perv wanting to get me in bed.

As he reached me he only said one thing,"cheating whore.'" Then he walked away disappearing in the mass. Why would he say that and what gave him that right?

I got home and again surprised at what I saw. My cat was crushed between the window and the frame. I ran over to see if it was still alive but it was too late. And it was my fault, I left the window open this morning. But why did it close, it never shut on its own before.

I called Mark to get a little comfort in the whole situation. He agreed to come over, plus he was going to bring pizza. A good start to recovery, in my mind. I ran into the bedroom to change clothes into something a little more comfortable and checked my makeup.

Mark rang the bell and I buzzed him in. At the door he had a pizza in one hand and a six pack in the other. He really thought of everything. He entered and put the food down and turned and gave me a hug. With the day I was having I really didn't want him to let go. It was a feeling I haven't felt in a long time. I looked up at him and he kissed me, he kissed me hard and for a long time. At that time light bulbs started to blow, first in the living room, then in the dining room. And an eerie coldness reclaimed the apartment like it did the night before.

Startled we broke our embrace and looked around to again find nothing. Then a book off the bookshelf flew off and hit Mark in the face. Blood started to appear on his otherwise flawless face. It got so cold we could see our breath, just like as if it was winter. Then the TV turned on and off repeatedly, as more books started flying off the shelves. We dodged the books to run into the bedroom but as we got there the door slammed in our faces. We turned to run for the front door and when we got there it would not open.

Scared to death we ran into the kitchen, first Mark then me but as we entered a knife flew off the counter and hit mark in the chest. He fell back into my hands but I could not hold his weight. We dropped to the floor and I looked at the glassy look on mark's face as he took his last breathes. The wound was fatal and he died right in my arms. I cried as things stopped flying around my head.

I went to call for an ambulance and before I got to the phone again Dan appeared in front of me. This time he wasn't in a mirror and I could not constitute this being my imagination. He looked at me and he was angry.

"Did you forget about me? You cheating whore. We are to get married soon and you're whoring around on me. What in the hell are you doing?" he said plain as day. All I could do is drop to my knees and cry as he hovered over me. "I knew I couldn't trust you. Now you must pay"

As my hysteria subsided I heard sirens getting closer to me. I looked up at Dan and pleaded for forgiveness.

"Now I will be sure you will not touch another man." Dan said in a voice that I never thought he could make. "You will now pay for all your indiscretions."

Then there was a pounding on the door and it flew open as police officers ran into the room. They rushed by me to find Mark dead on the floor. I couldn't even speak as they arrested me for murder. I was convicted a year later and now I have to spend the rest of my life in jail without parole. Dan still comes to me almost daily, mostly as I am about to fall asleep. The torment of this has broken me, and I know what I have to do.

I tied the sheet to the light fixture in my cell and the other around my neck. All I have to do is kick the chair away. Dan watched as I was about to end my life. He just smiled, almost like he was approving. Then I kicked the chair away and the lights went out. Finally I was at peace......I don't know about Dan and I don't care.

ABOUT THE AUTHOR

Jason Hess was born outside Chicago in 1969 and raised there through out his life. Many strange accounts happened to him and later in life he started to research and investigates paranormal experiences. Although his writings are purely fiction, he uses some of his findings in his works. Through out the paranormal community many skeptic claim true stories to be fictions so he just cut to the chase and made it the way he did.

As more experience come around Jason will take notes and continue to write short stories. So don't worry, more will soon come.